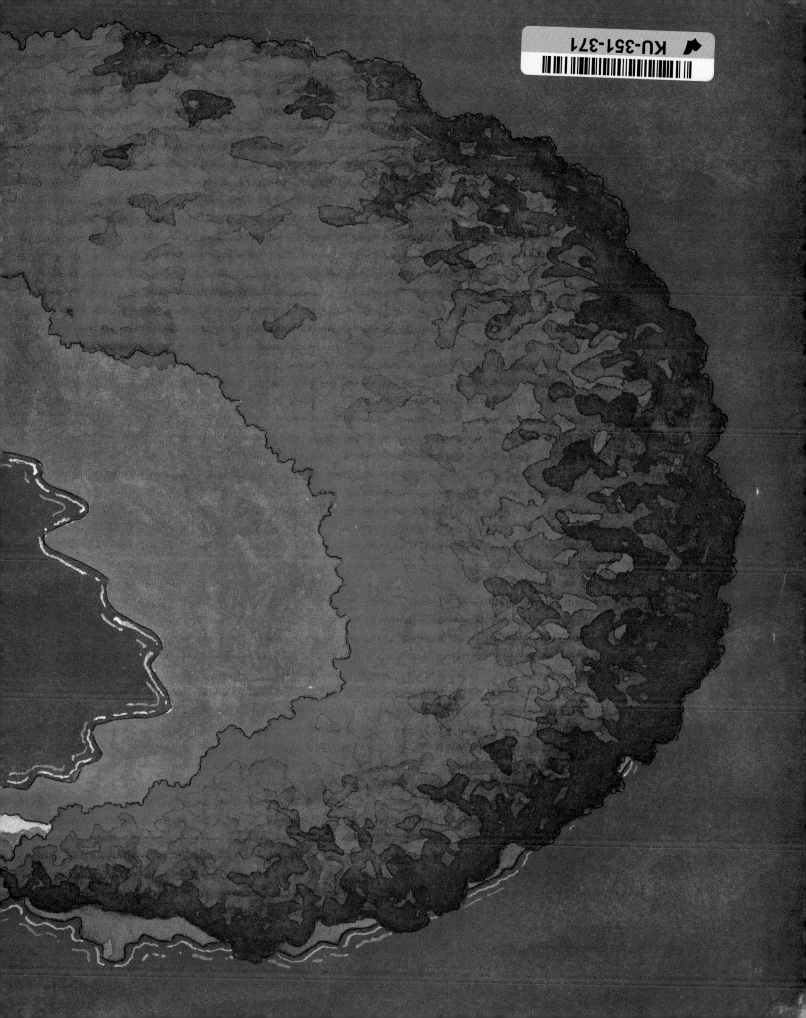

For Rachel, Max and Laura, my own pirate crew. – J.E.

For Gary. – A.R.

OXFORD
UNIVERSITY PRESS

Great Clarendon Street, Oxford OX2 6DP

Oxford University Press is a department of the University of Oxford.
It furthers the University's objective of excellence in research, scholarship,
and education by publishing worldwide in

Oxford New York
Auckland Cape Town Dar es Salaam Hong Kong Karachi
Kuala Lumpur Madrid Melbourne Mexico City Nairobi
New Delhi Shanghai Taipei Toronto

With offices in
Argentina Austria Brazil Chile Czech Republic France Greece
Guatemala Hungary Italy Japan Poland Portugal Singapore
South Korea Switzerland Thailand Turkey Ukraine Vietnam

Oxford is a registered trade mark of Oxford University Press
in the UK and in certain other countries

British Library Cataloguing in Publication Data available

ISBN-13: 978-0-19-279119-1 (Hardback)
ISBN-10: 0-19-279119-2 (Hardback)
ISBN-13: 978-0-19-272558-5 (Paperback)
ISBN-10: 0-19-272558-0 (Paperback)

2 4 6 8 10 9 7 5 3 1

Printed in Singapore

You can find out more about Jonathan Emmett's
books by visiting his website at
www.scribblestreet.co.uk

Jonathan Emmett
and Adrian Reynolds

OXFORD

UNIVERSITY PRESS

If we had a sailboat,
if we had a racing yacht,

we could sail across the ocean,

we could head for somewhere hot.

We could hoist the Jolly Roger
and become a pirate crew.

We could find a desert island

and some buried treasure, too!

And if we had a steam train
we could speed along the track,

we could wave to other steam trains
and their drivers would wave back.

We could journey through the jungle,

we could race across the plain,

and we'd fight off all the bandits

when they tried to rob our train.

And if we had a rocket
we could travel to the stars,

we could float around in orbit –
we might even land on Mars.

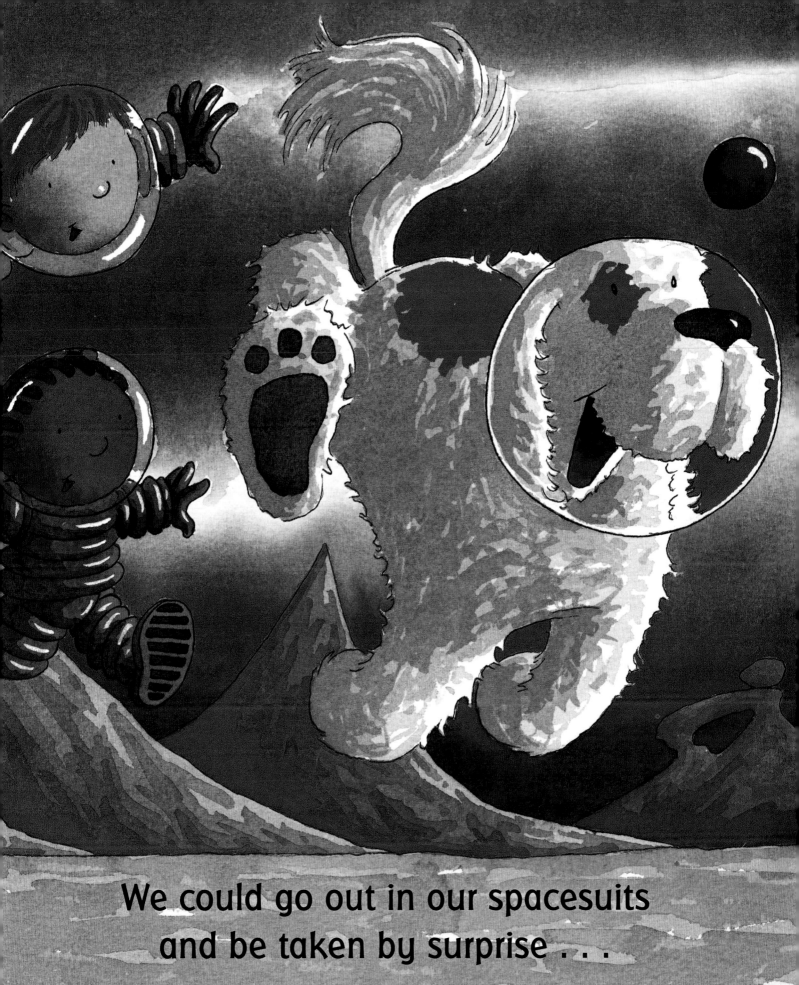

We could go out in our spacesuits
and be taken by surprise . . .

by a crazy-looking Martian

who had far too many eyes!

But we don't have a rocket
or a steam train or a yacht,

but we HAVE got each other –
and that's better than the lot!